**DERRYDALE BOOKS**
**New York**

This 1984 edition is published by Derrydale Books,
distributed by Crown Publishers Inc.
© Peter Haddock Ltd, Bridlington, U.K.
Printed in Hungary

ISBN 0-517-43877-1
HGFEDCBA

# AN AMAZING ALPHABET

## By John Patience

# Aa

Anxious animals in an anchored ark.

Busy
baker with a
batch of
bread - oops!
banana skin.

# Bb

# Cc

Crazy
cat in a
car
causing
cock
concern.

David and the dainty dragon dancing in the daisies.

Dd

# Ee

Enormous
elephant
eating
eggs.

Fairies, flowers, feather and frog.

**Ff**

# Gg

Goose
girl
greeting
gentle
giant.

Hasty
hare
helping
himself to
honey from a
hive.

# Hh

# Ii

Indian
imagining
incredible
ice-cream.

# Jj

Jolly
jester
juggling
jell-O.

# Kk

Kitten catching the kind king's kite.

**Large lion** and **little lizard licking lollipops.**

Ll

# Mm

Moon,
mushroom and
many
merry-making
mice.

# Nn

Nest of
noisy
nightingales.

# Oo

One
odd
old
owl.

Parrot
perching on the
peg-legged
pirate.

# Pp

# Qq

Queasy
queen
quarreling with
quacky duck.

# Rr

Rhinoceros in a
rocking chair
reading to a
robin.

# Ss

Sailor
shrews
sail the
salty seas.

**Trolls** gathering **tasty treats** for their **tea**.

Tt

# Uu

Unusual
unicorn
under an
umbrella.

# Vv

Valuable
vase
vexing
vole with
violin.

# Ww

Witch and wizard waving wands.

# XYZ

Xylophone　　Yak　　Zebra

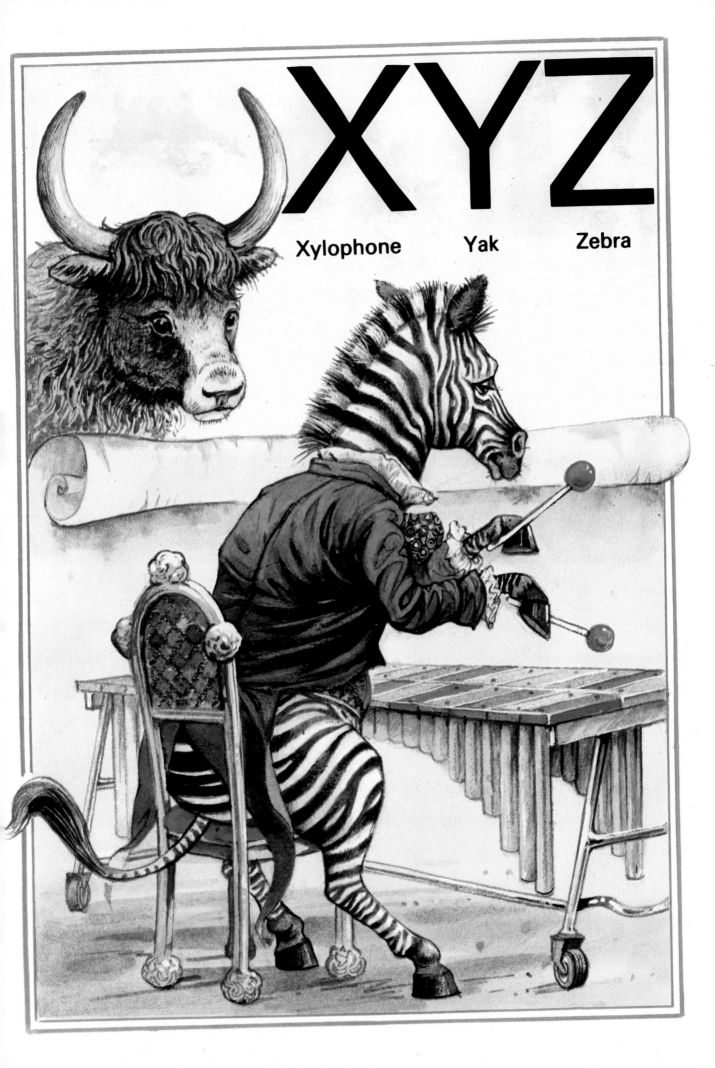